YOU CAN BE ANYTHING!

YOU CAN BE ANYTHING!

Based on the comics by
Charles M. Schulz

RP|KIDS
PHILADELPHIA • LONDON

9 8 7 6 5 4 3 2 1
Digit on the right indicates the number of this printing

Library of Congress Control Number: 2008933259

ISBN 978-0-7624-3583-8

Text adapted by Megan E. Bryant
Art adapted by Tom Brannon
Design by Frances J. Soo Ping Chow

Running Press Kids
an imprint of Running Press Book Publishers
2300 Chestnut Street
Philadelphia, PA 19103-4371

Visit us on the web!
www.runningpress.com
www.Snoopy.com

Just like Snoopy, what you can achieve
is limited only by your imagination.
YOU CAN BE ANYTHING!

You can be a
LEADER...

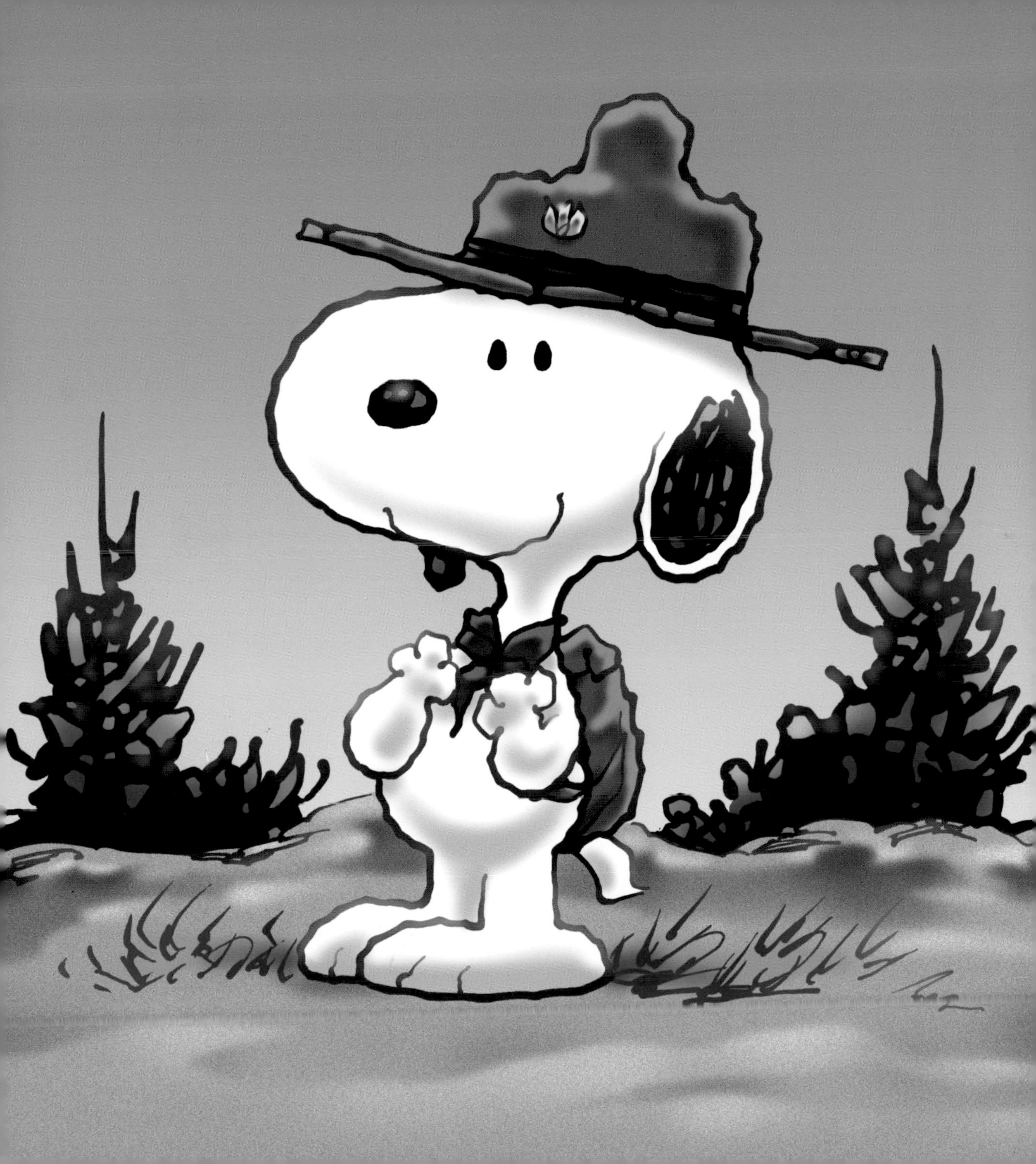

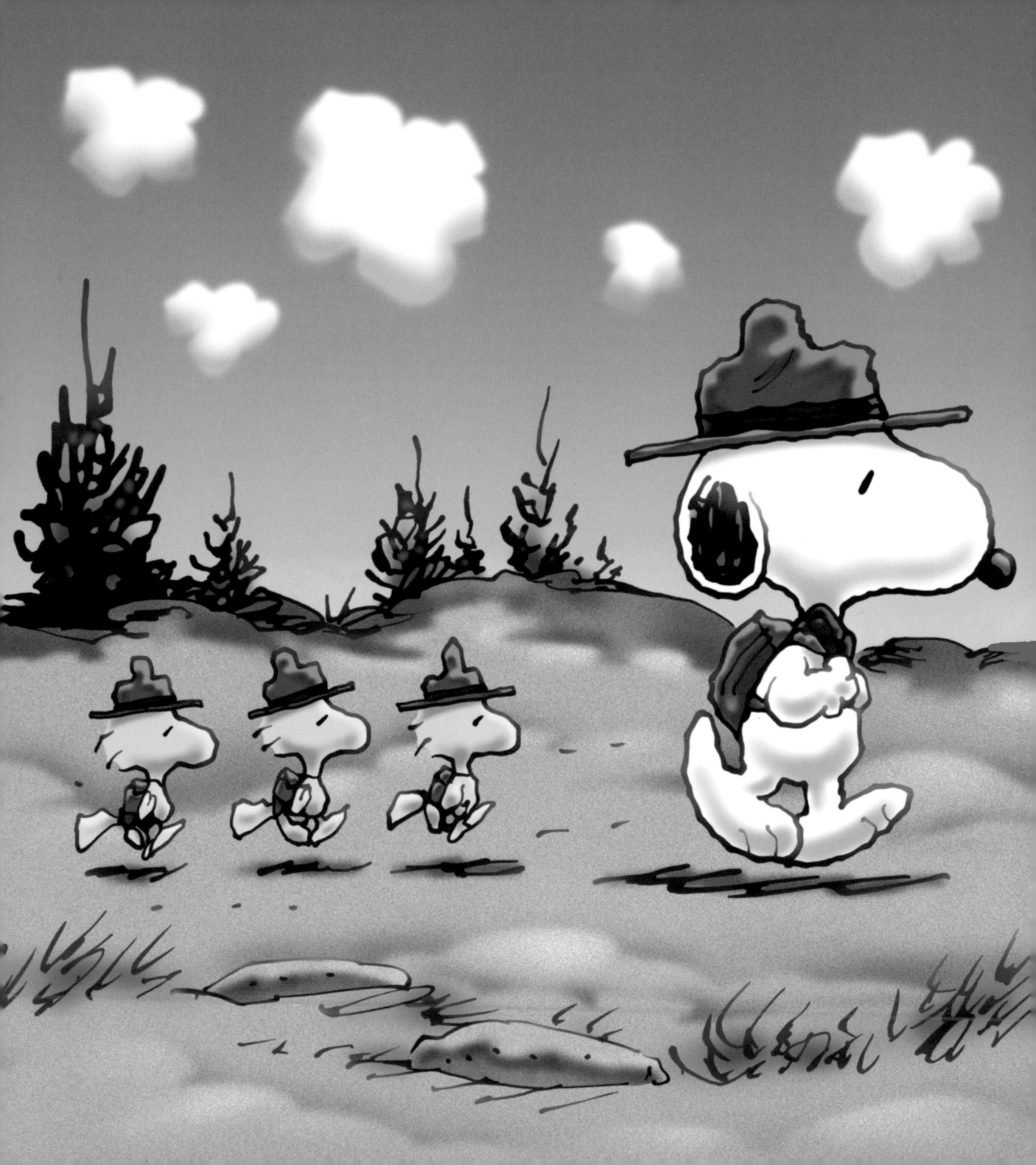

Here's the
world famous

BEAGLE
SCOUT

leading his troop
on a hike.

Here's

BLACKBEAGLE

the world famous pirate,
leading his scurvy
band ashore.

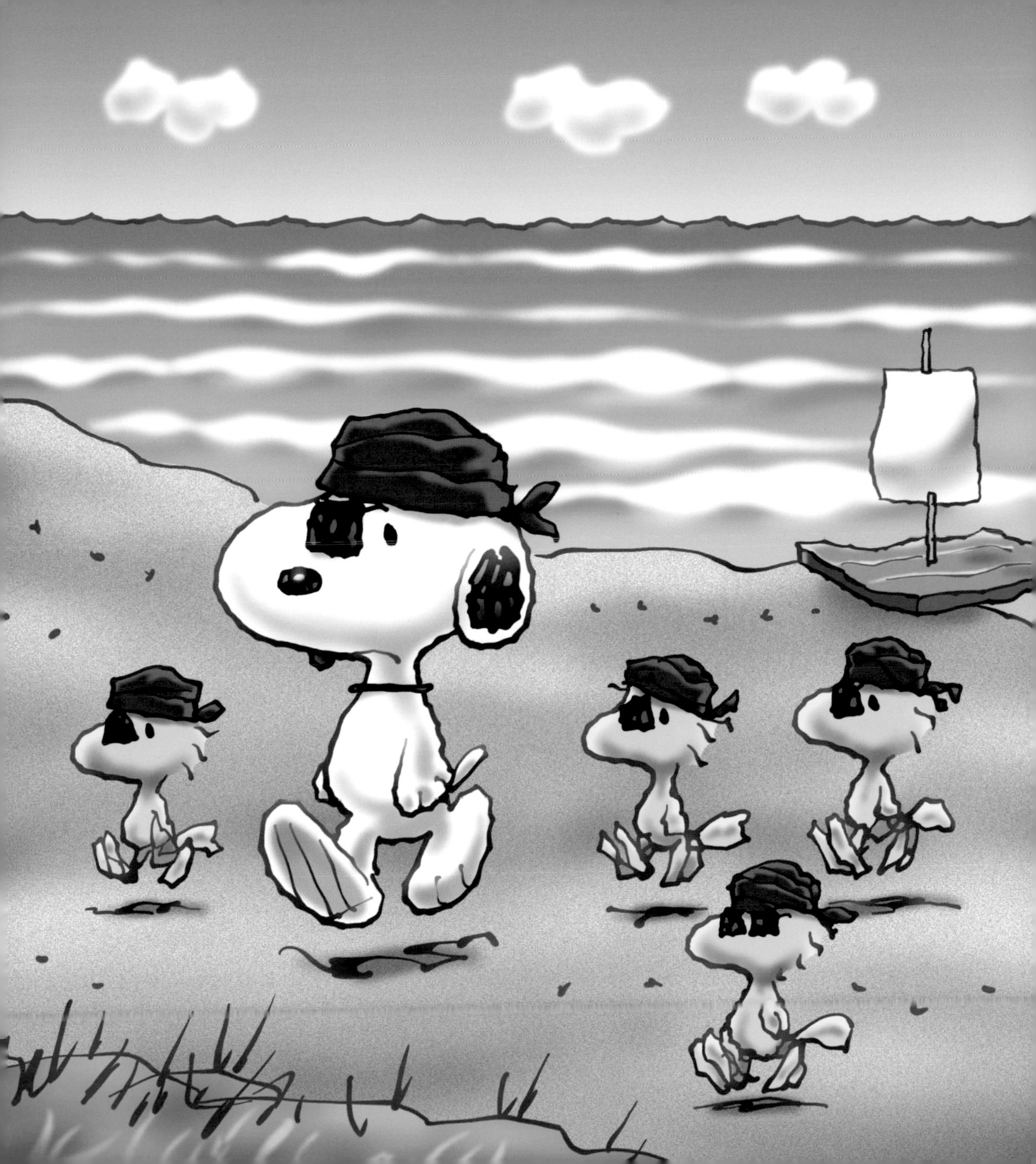

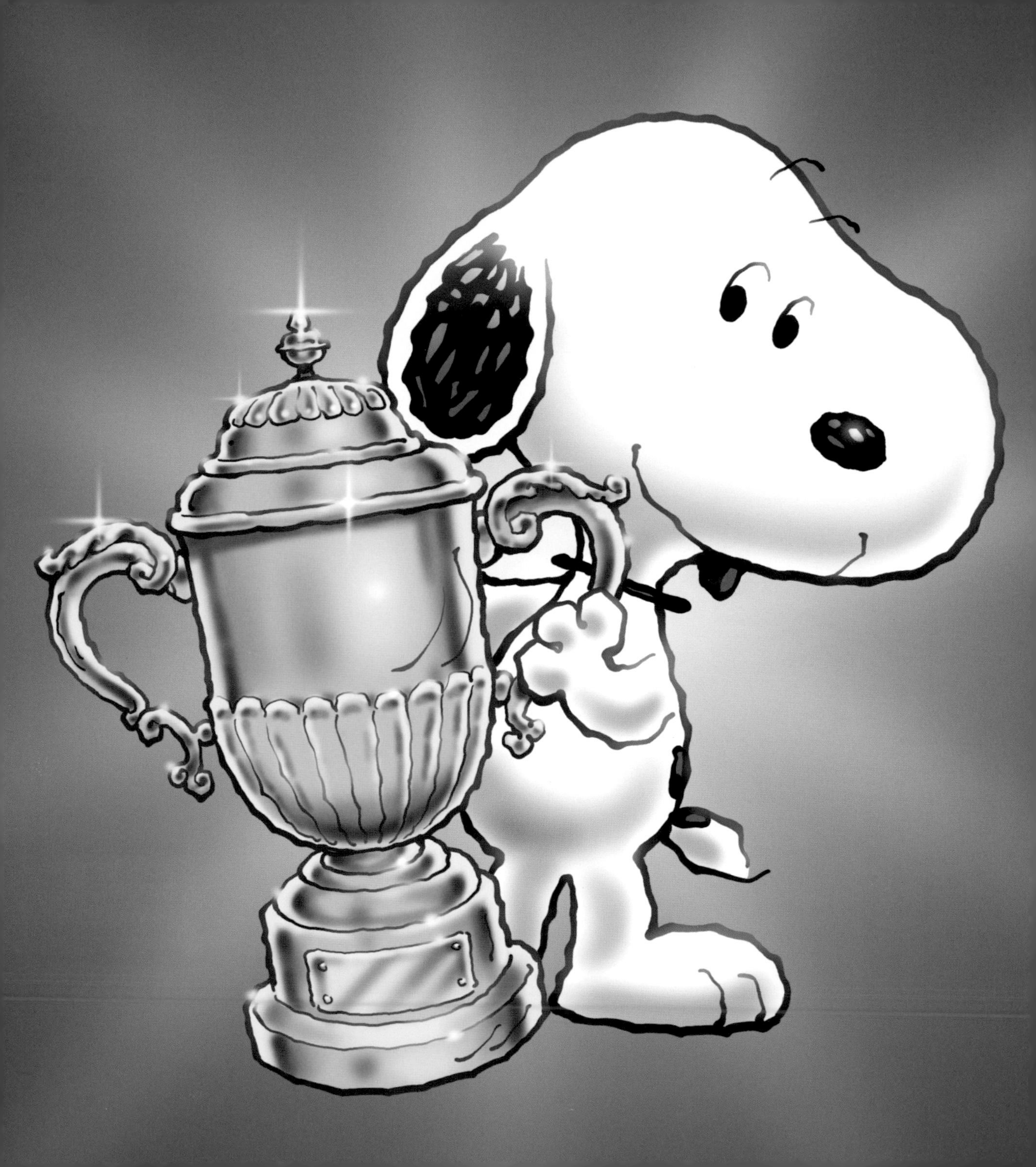

You can be a
SPORTS STAR...

And become a world famous
HOCKEY PLAYER

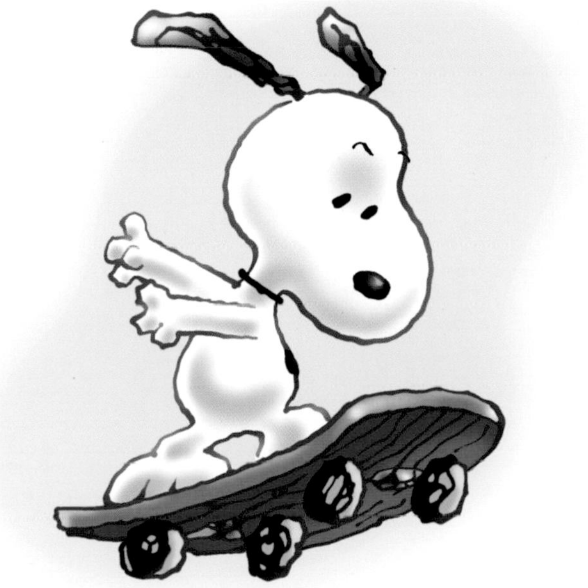

Or
JOE
SKATEBOARD

Or
A SURFER

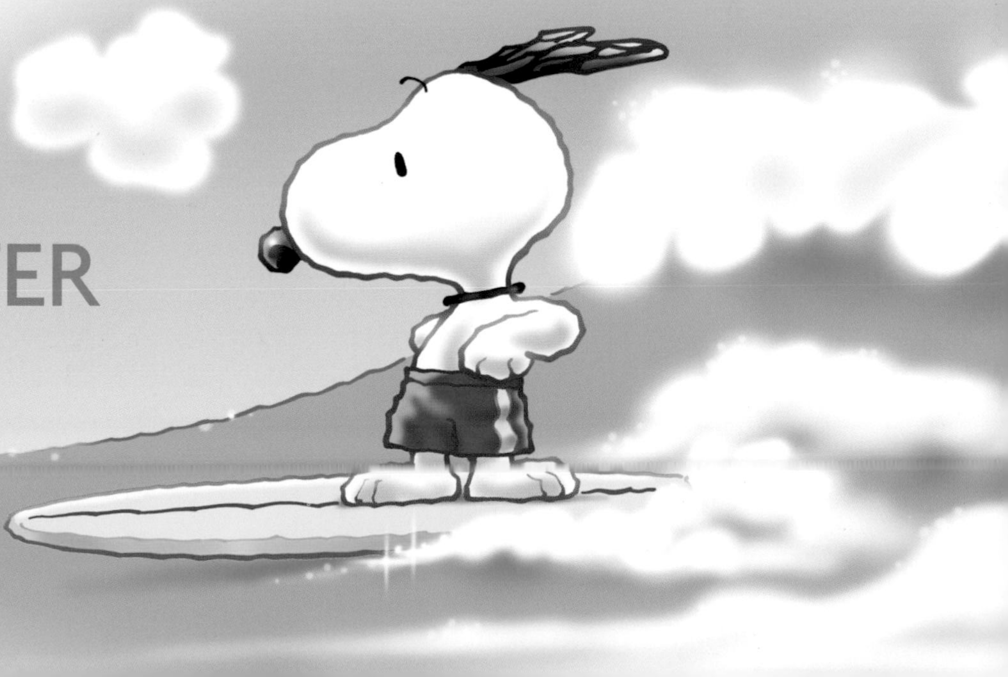

Or a
BASEBALL
PLAYER

Or a
TENNIS PRO

Or you can become a world famous

SKIER

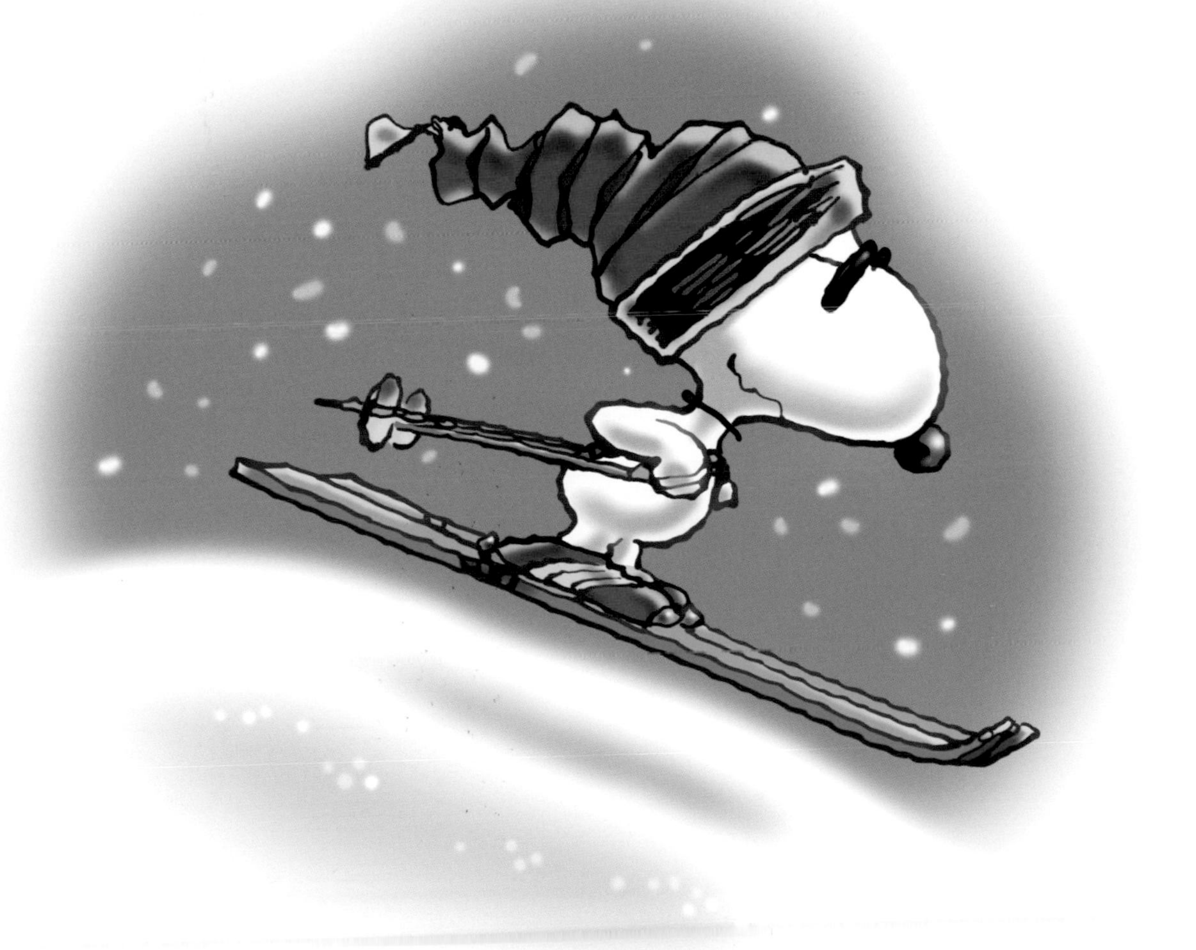

Or a
BOWLER

Or a
GOLF PRO

Or a
SWIMMER

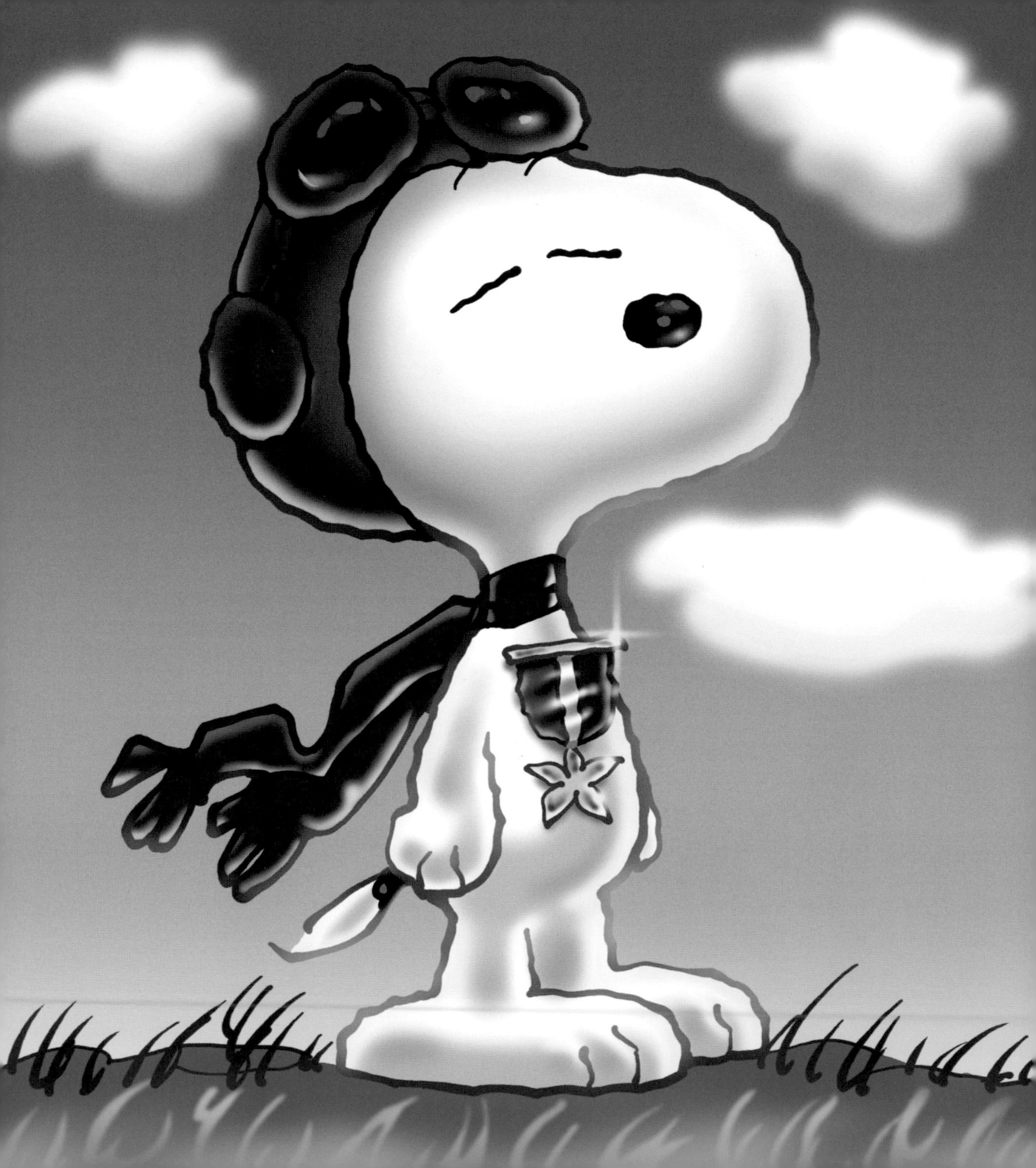

You can be a
HERO...

Here's the
WORLD WAR II FLYING ACE
zooming through the air searching for the Red Baron.

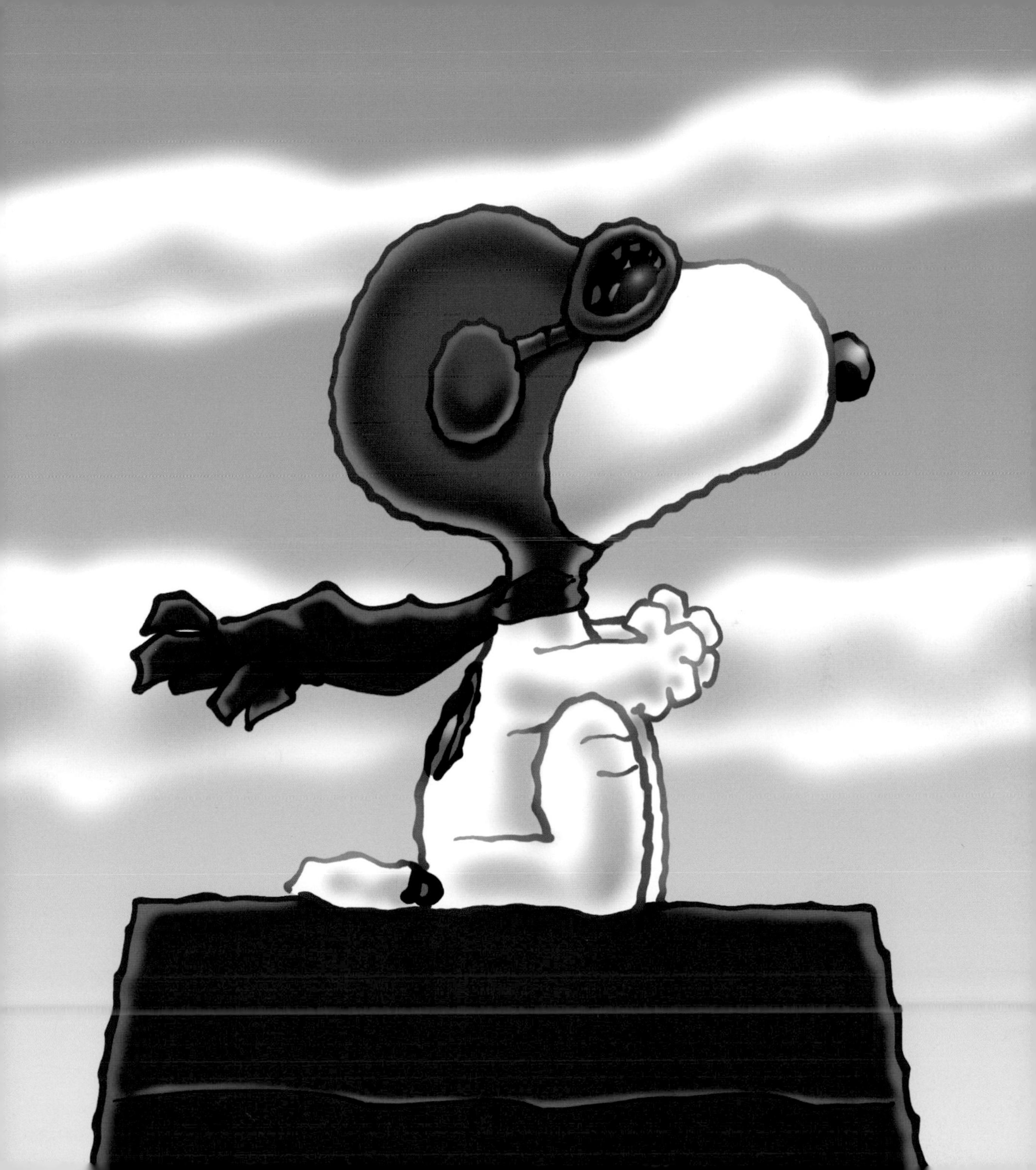

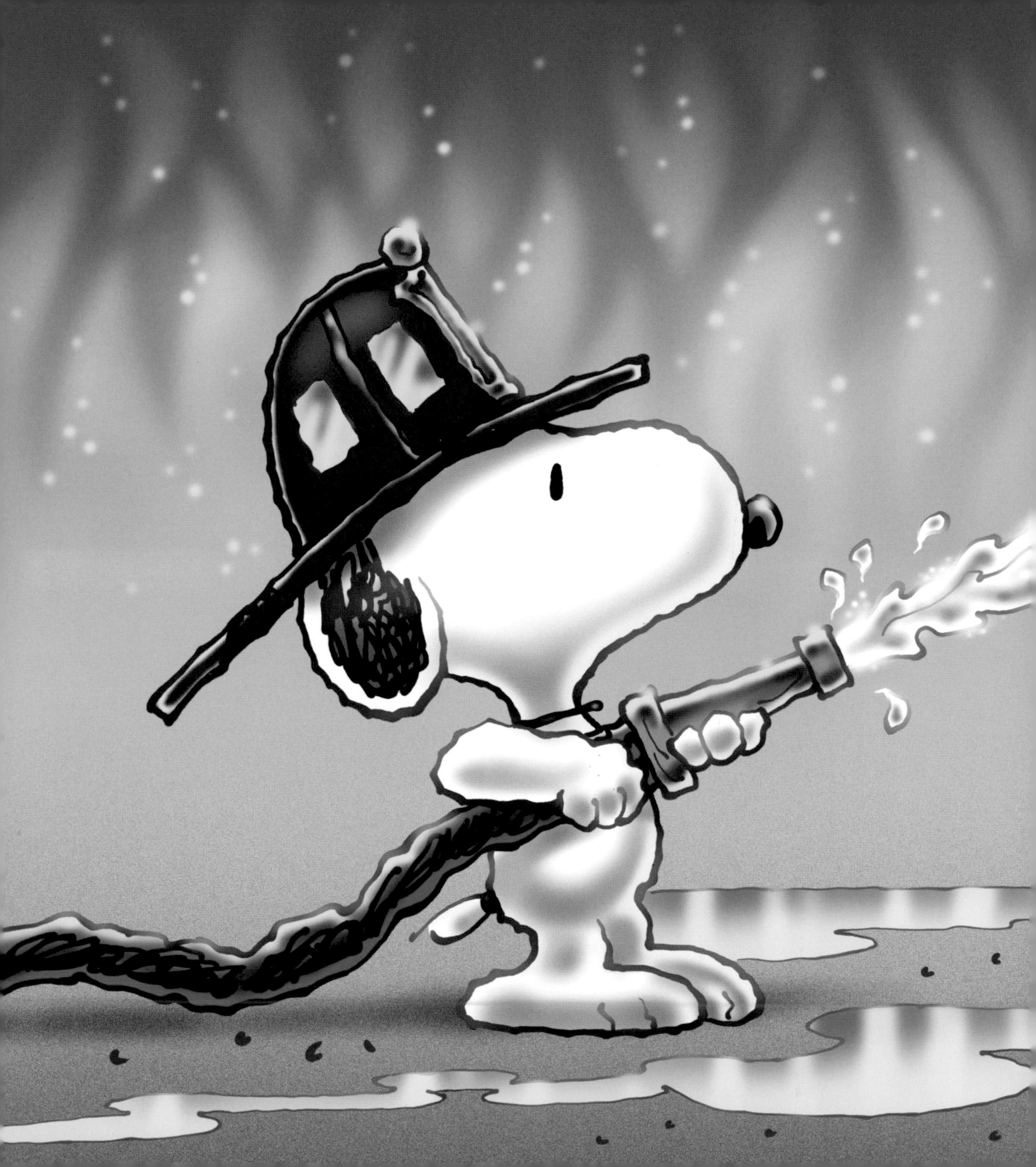

Here's
the world famous
FIRE FIGHTER.

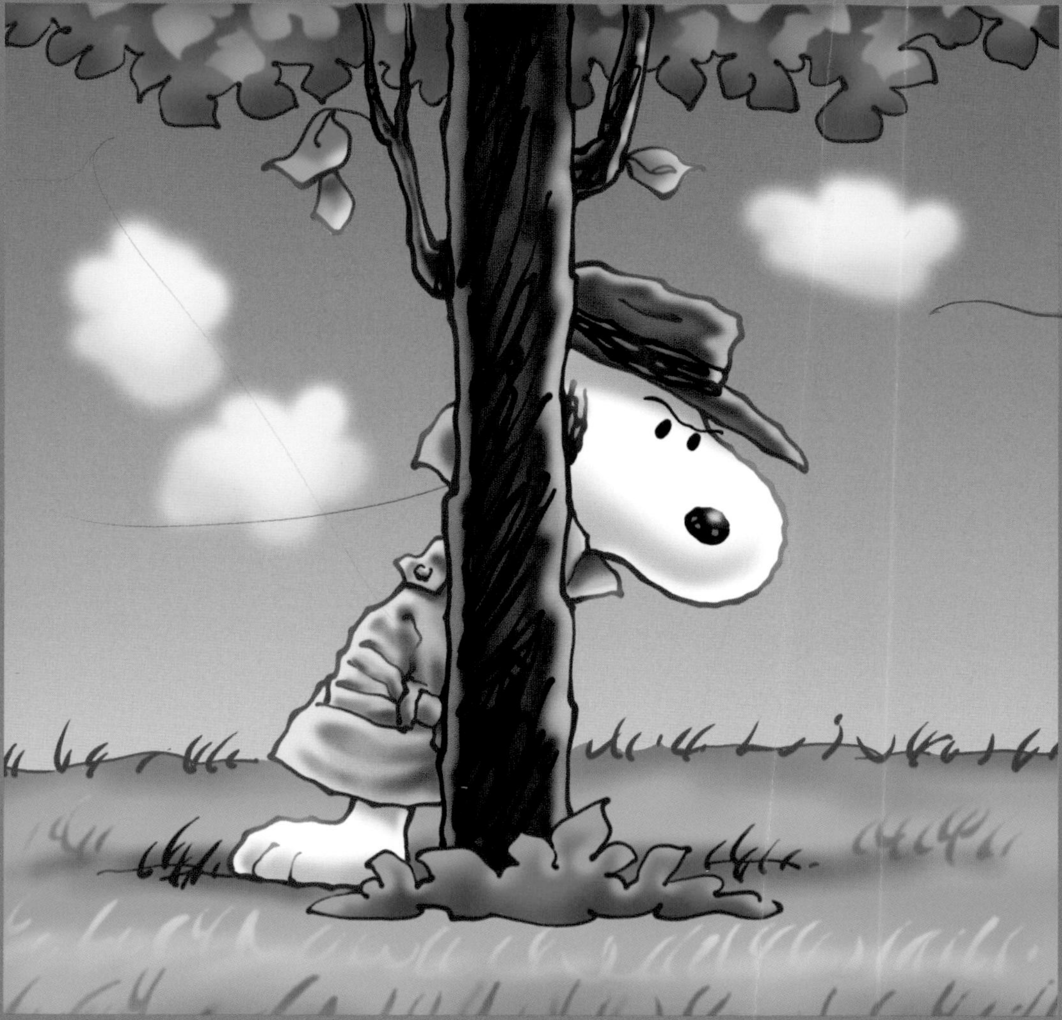

Here's the

SECRET AGENT

carrying out his dangerous mission.

And here's the

FIRST BEAGLE
ON THE MOON!

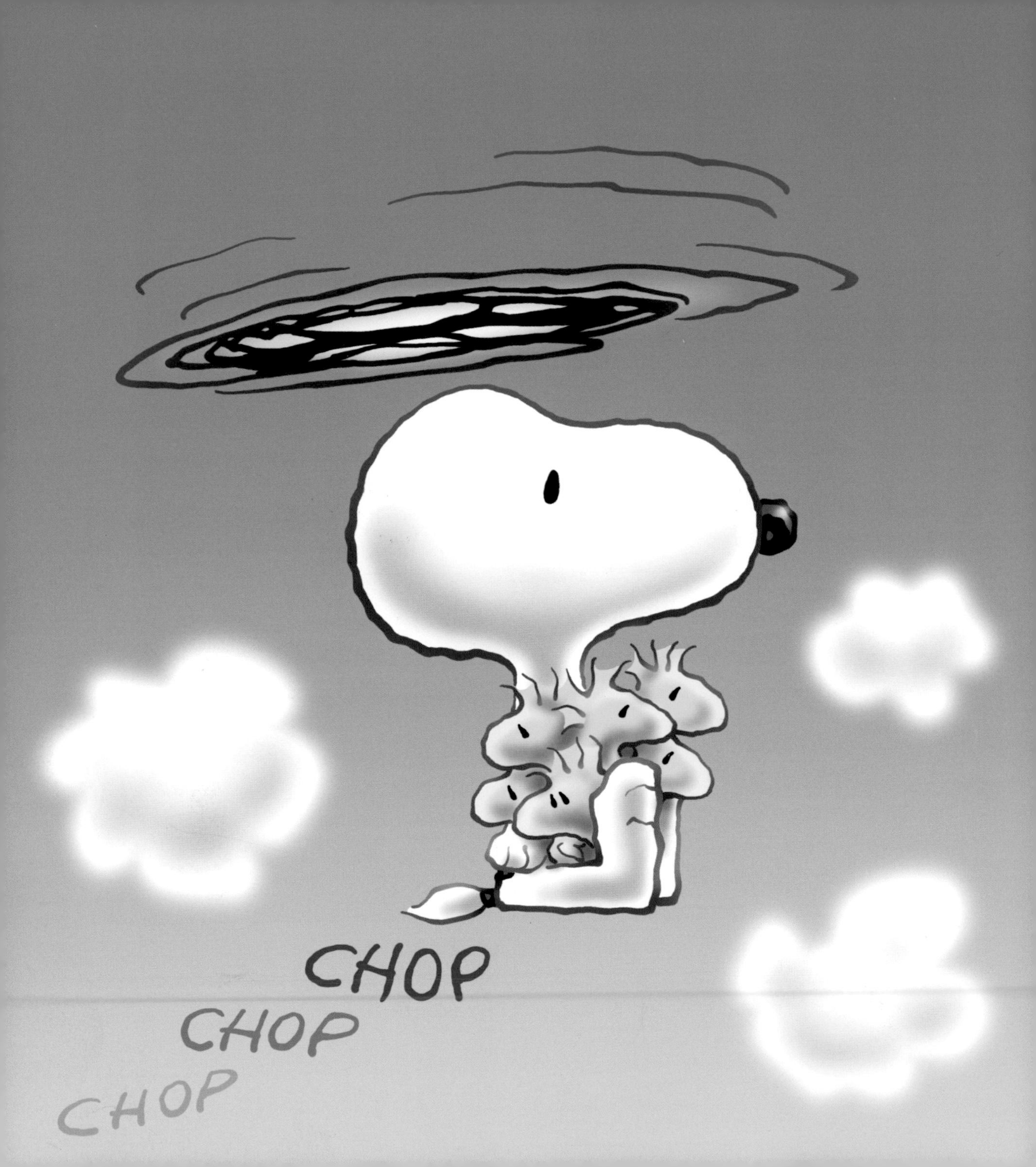
CHOP
CHOP
CHOP

Here's the

RESCUE

HELICOPTER

on an important mission…

(the helicopter is
dangerously overloaded.)

Or you can
have a
CAREER...

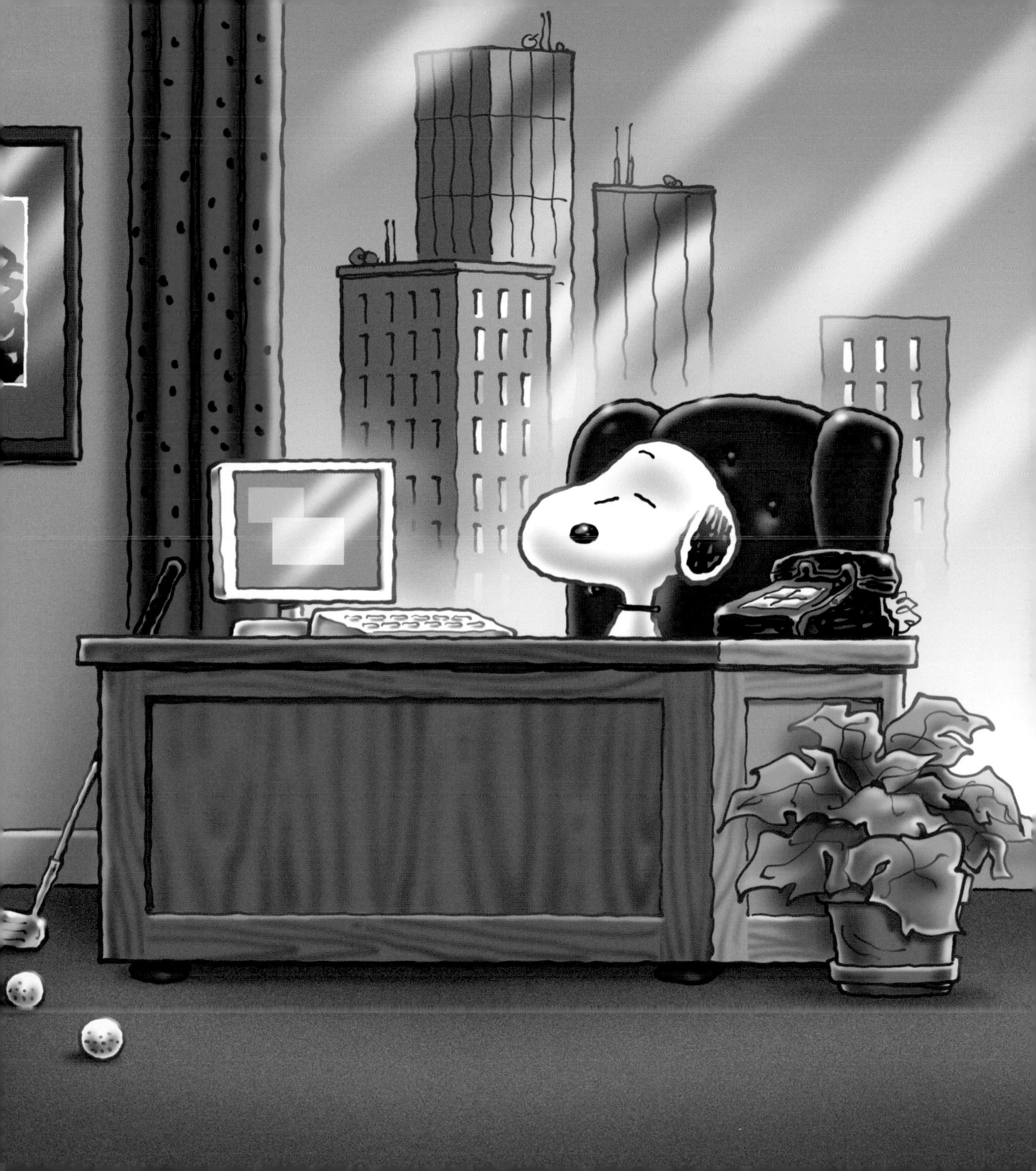

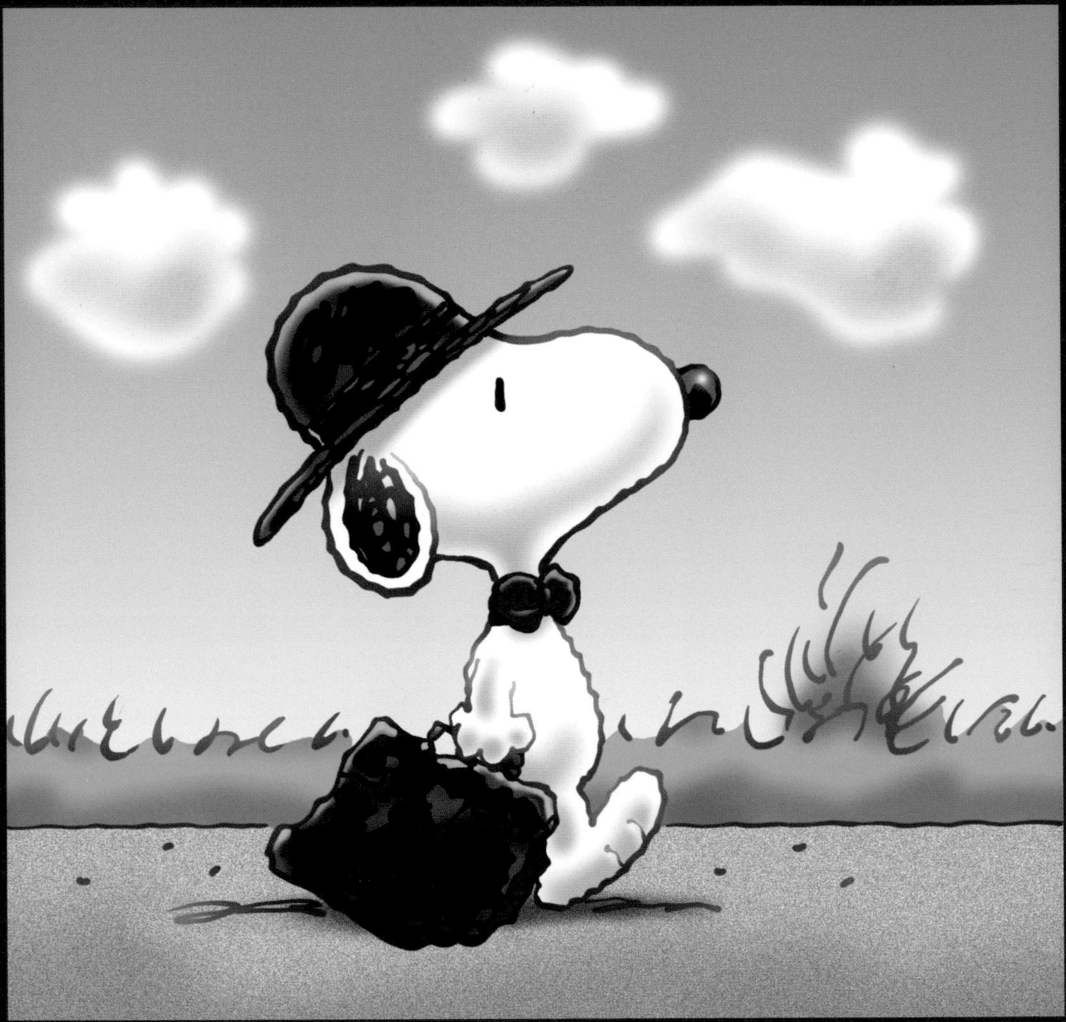

Here's the world famous

LAWYER

leaving the courthouse.

Here's the world famous

GROCERY CLERK

working at the checkout counter…
(actually, there aren't more than a dozen
world-famous grocery clerks.)

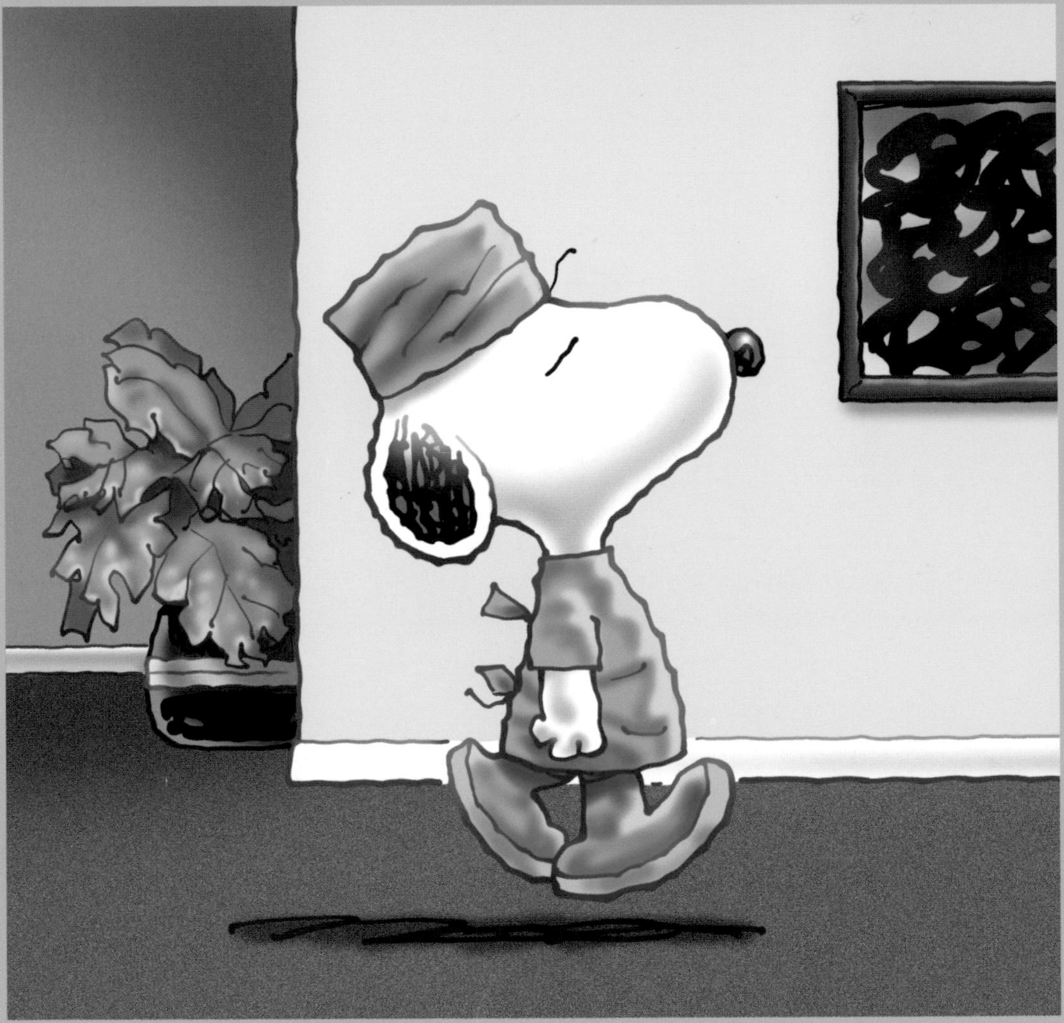

Here's the world famous

SURGEON

on his way to the operating room.

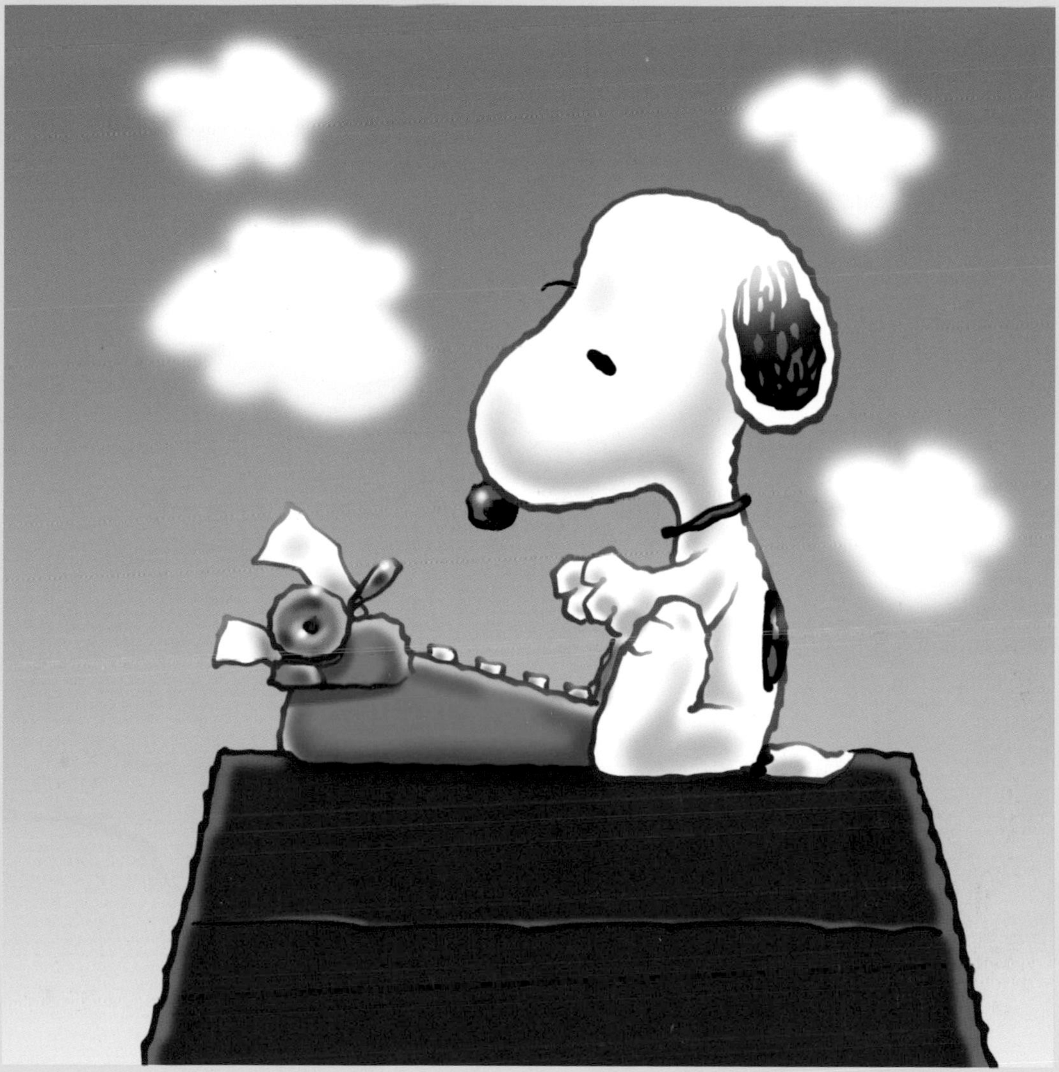

And here's the world famous

LITERARY ACE.

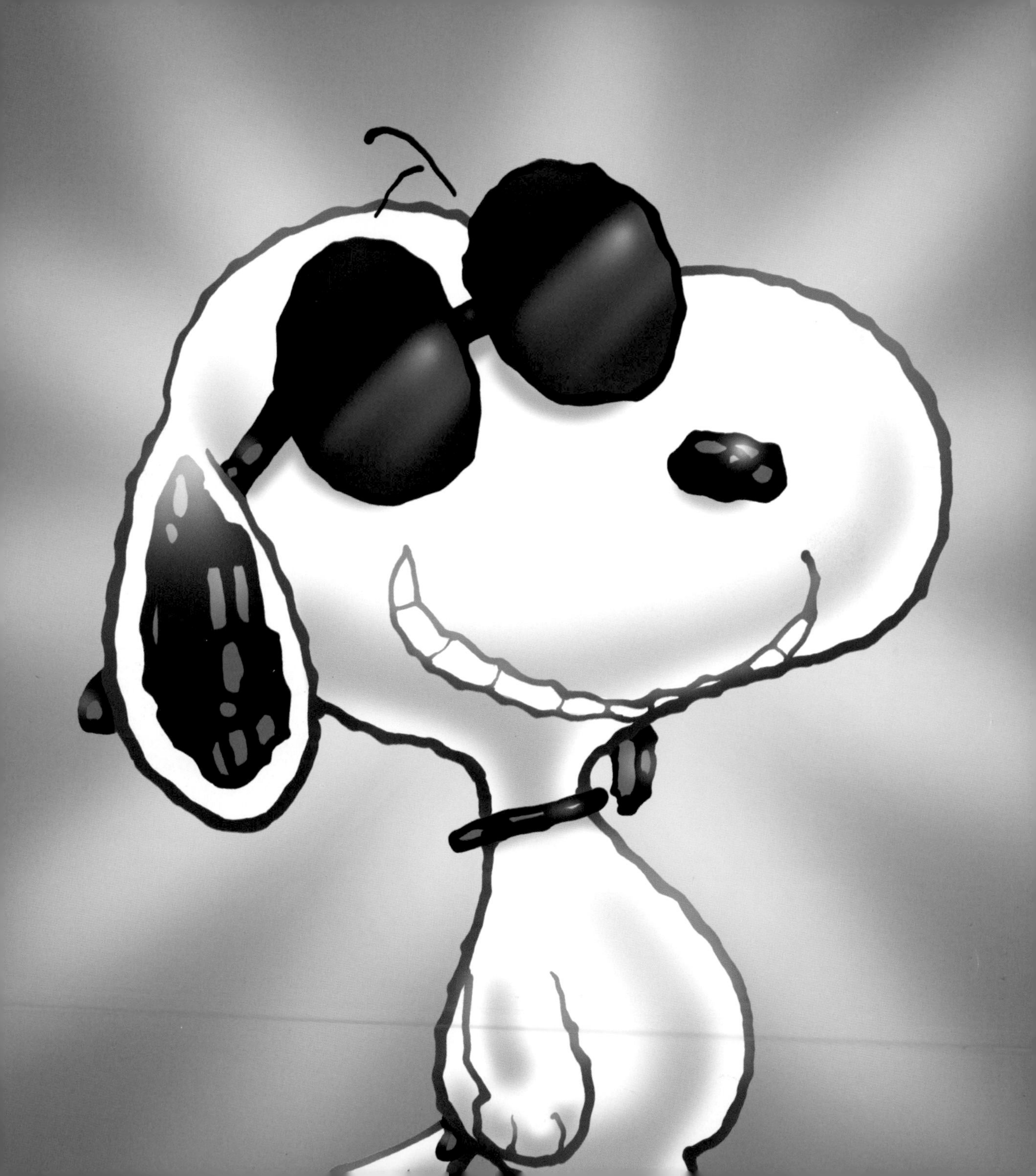

Or you can
be just

PLAIN

COOL…

Here's
JOE COOL
hanging around
the student union.

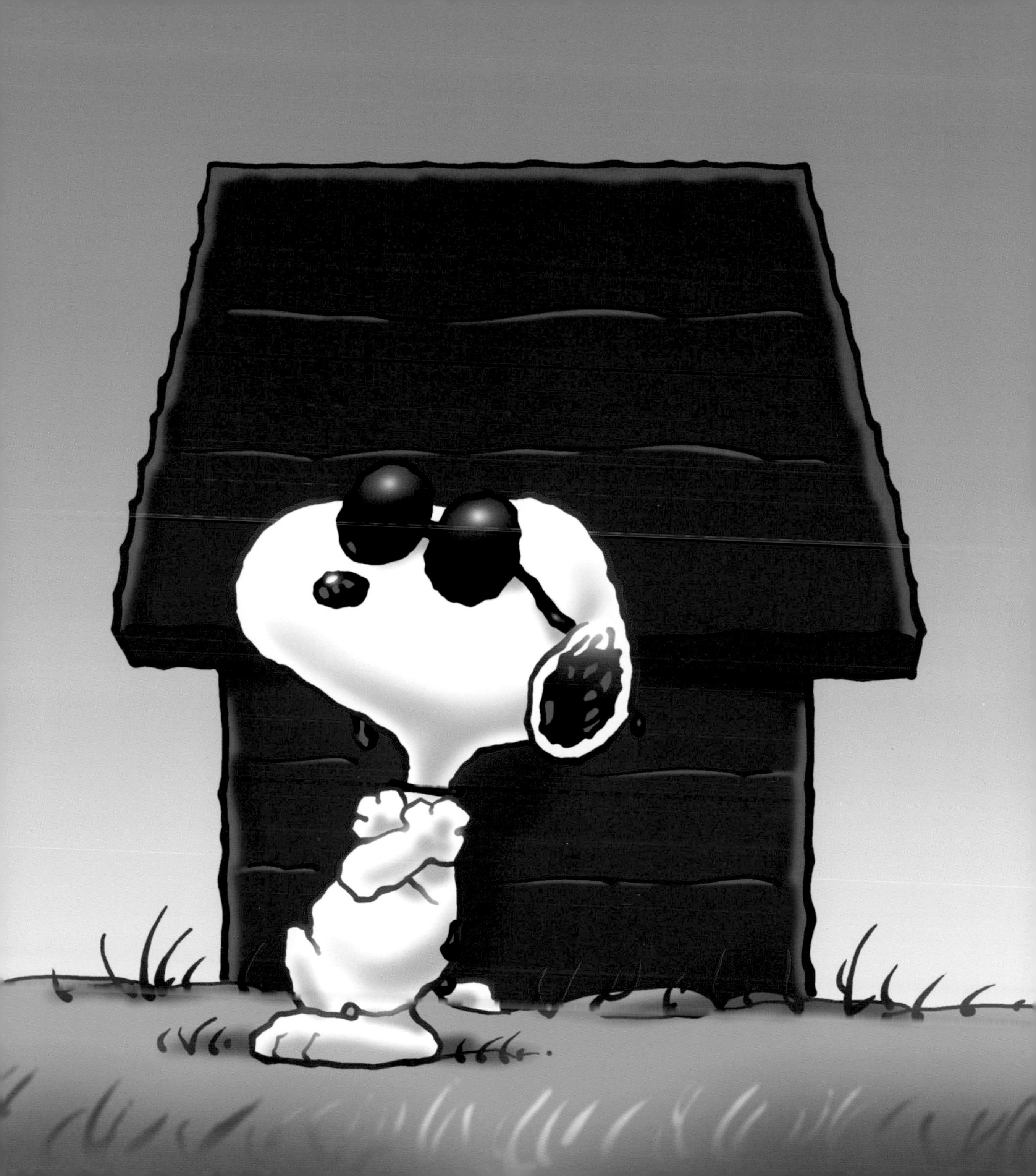

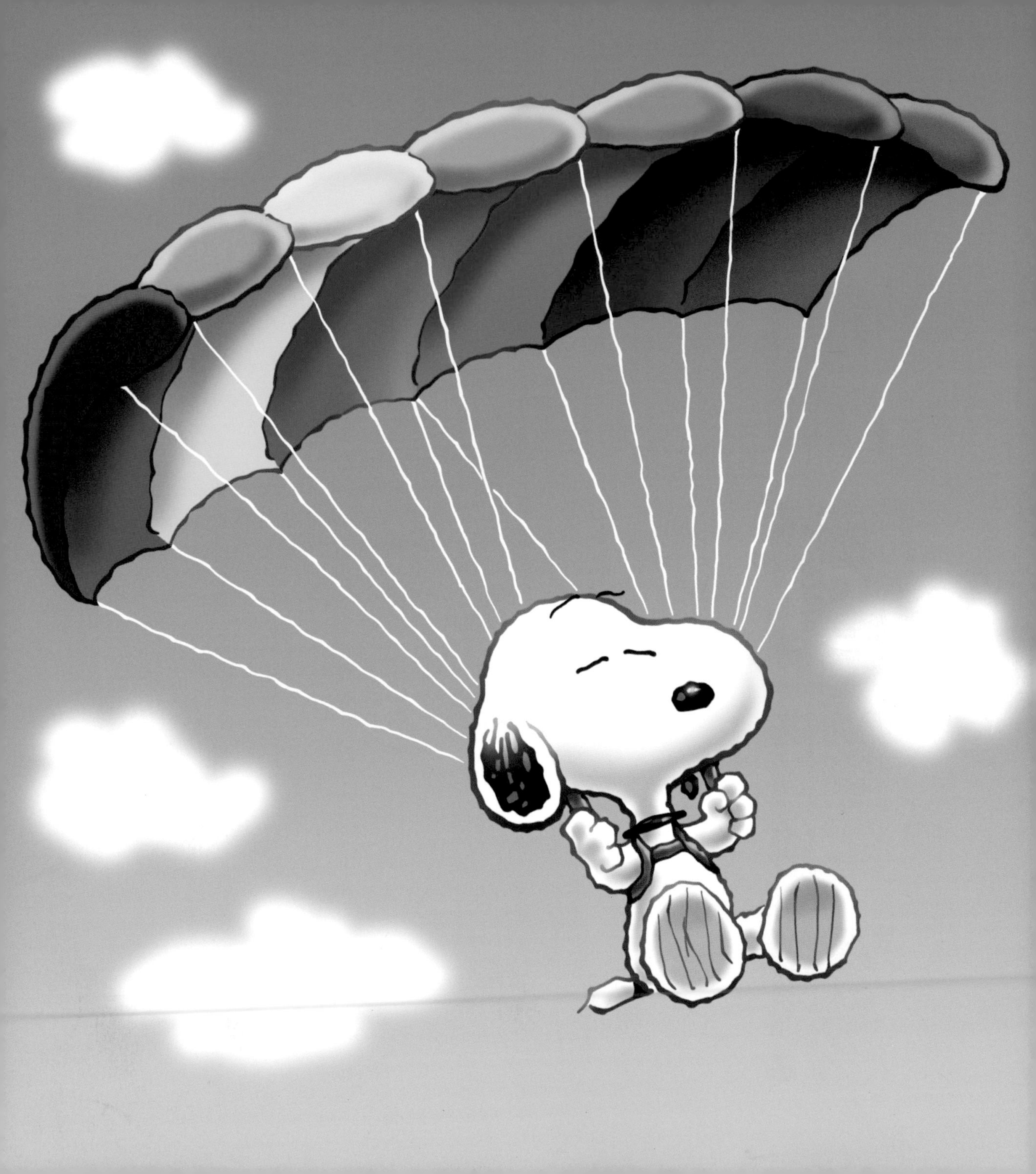

SNOOPY
ISN'T AFRAID
to try anything!

Here's
JOE PREPPY

And the
world famous
DISCO
DANCER

And the
world famous
ROLLER DERBY
STAR

Here's
PUNK
BEAGLE

And
JOE
GRUNGE

And
JOE BUNGEE

And here's…
FLASHBEAGLE!

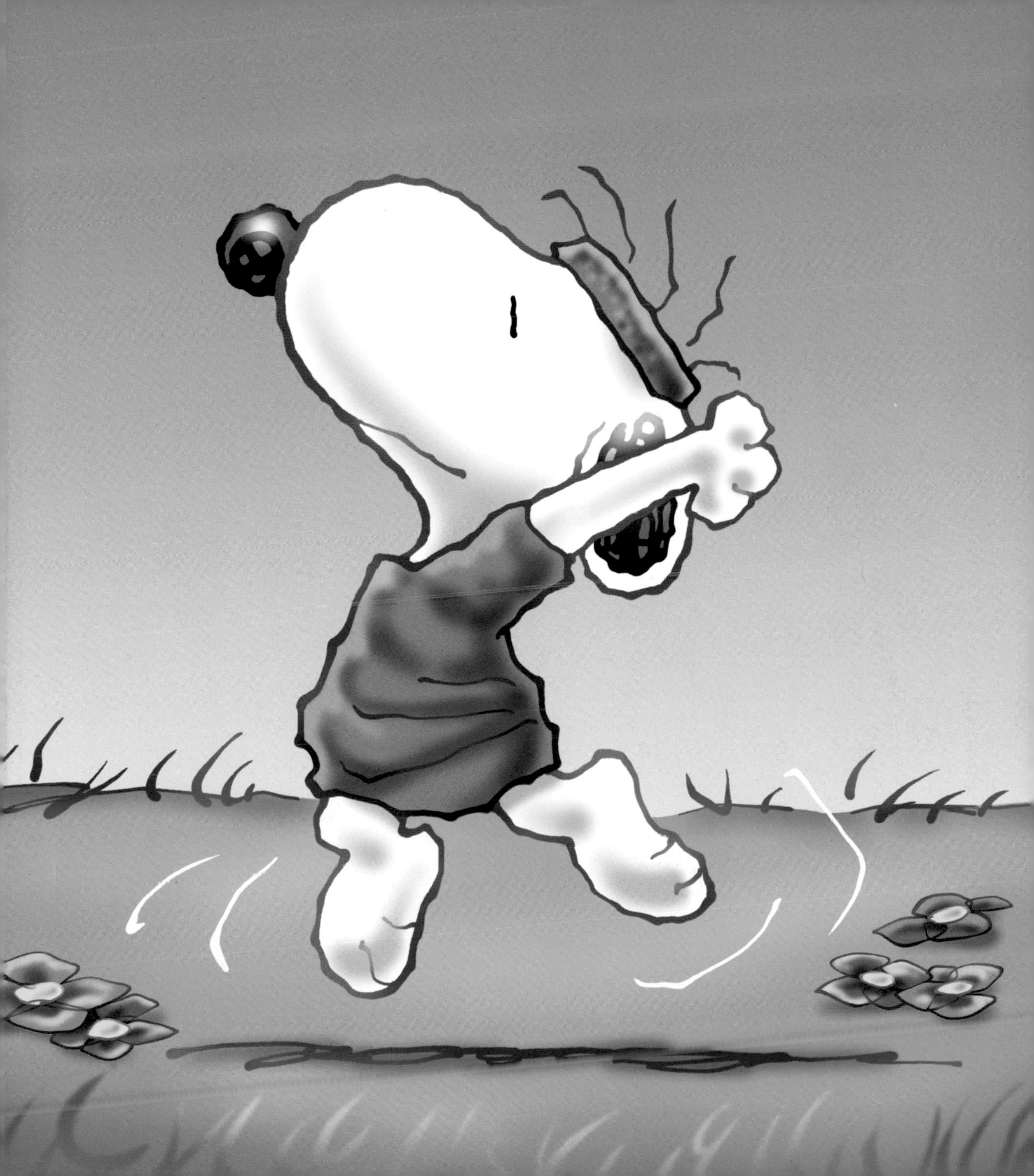

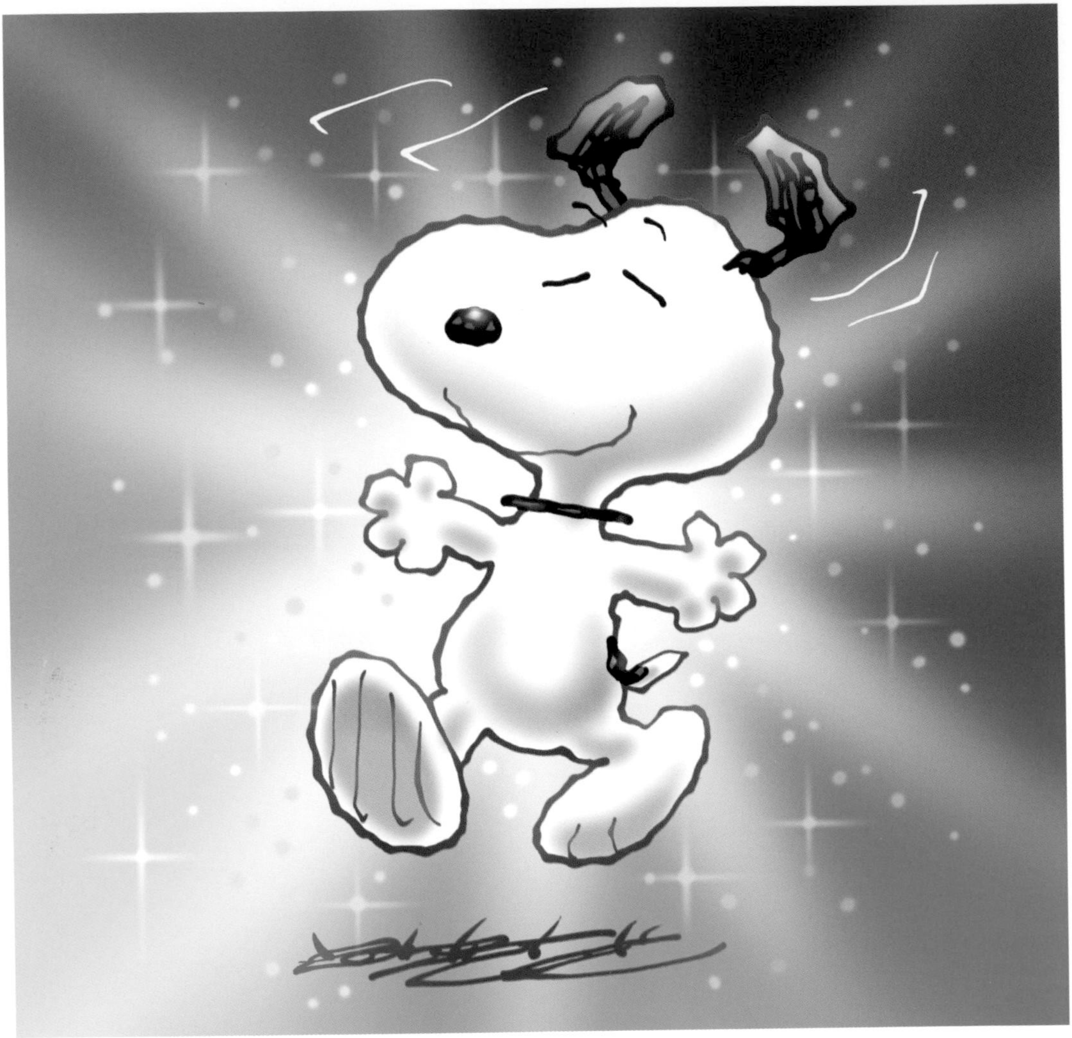

Be a leader, be a hero, be smart,
and be different—because just like Snoopy,

YOU CAN BE ANYTHING!

LOST AND FOUND

I wish, I wish
With all my heart
To fly with dragons
In a land apart.

By Margaret Snyder
Illustrated by Don Williams
Based on the characters by Ron Rodecker

Visit Dragon Tales on the Web at www.dragontales.com
Watch us on PBS!

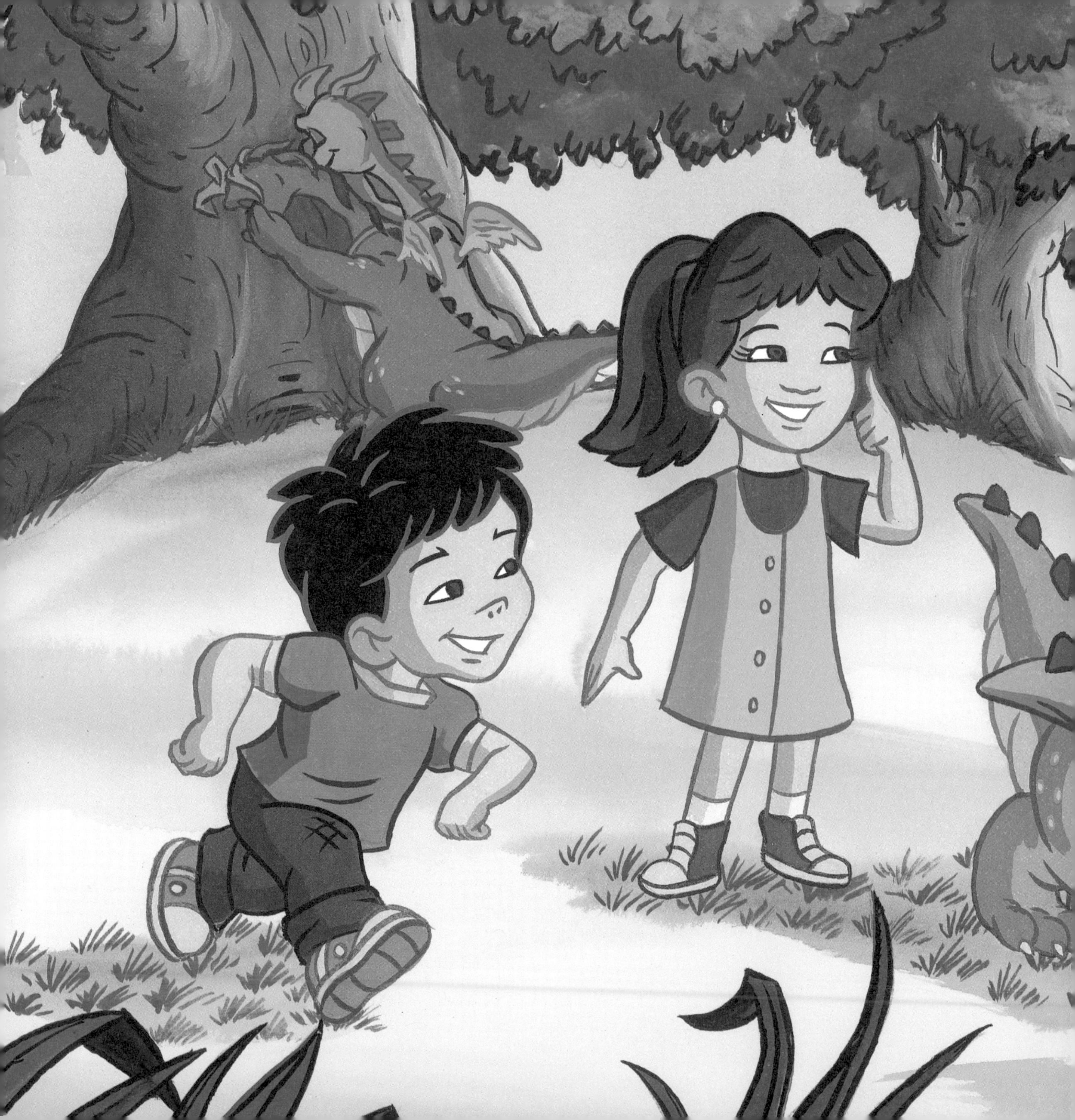

Emmy loved playing hide-and-seek in Dragon Land, but it sure was hard to hide from a two-headed dragon.

"Pick a good spot to hide, everyone," Wheezie sang out. She and Zak closed their eyes and began to count.

This time, Emmy was determined to be the last one found.

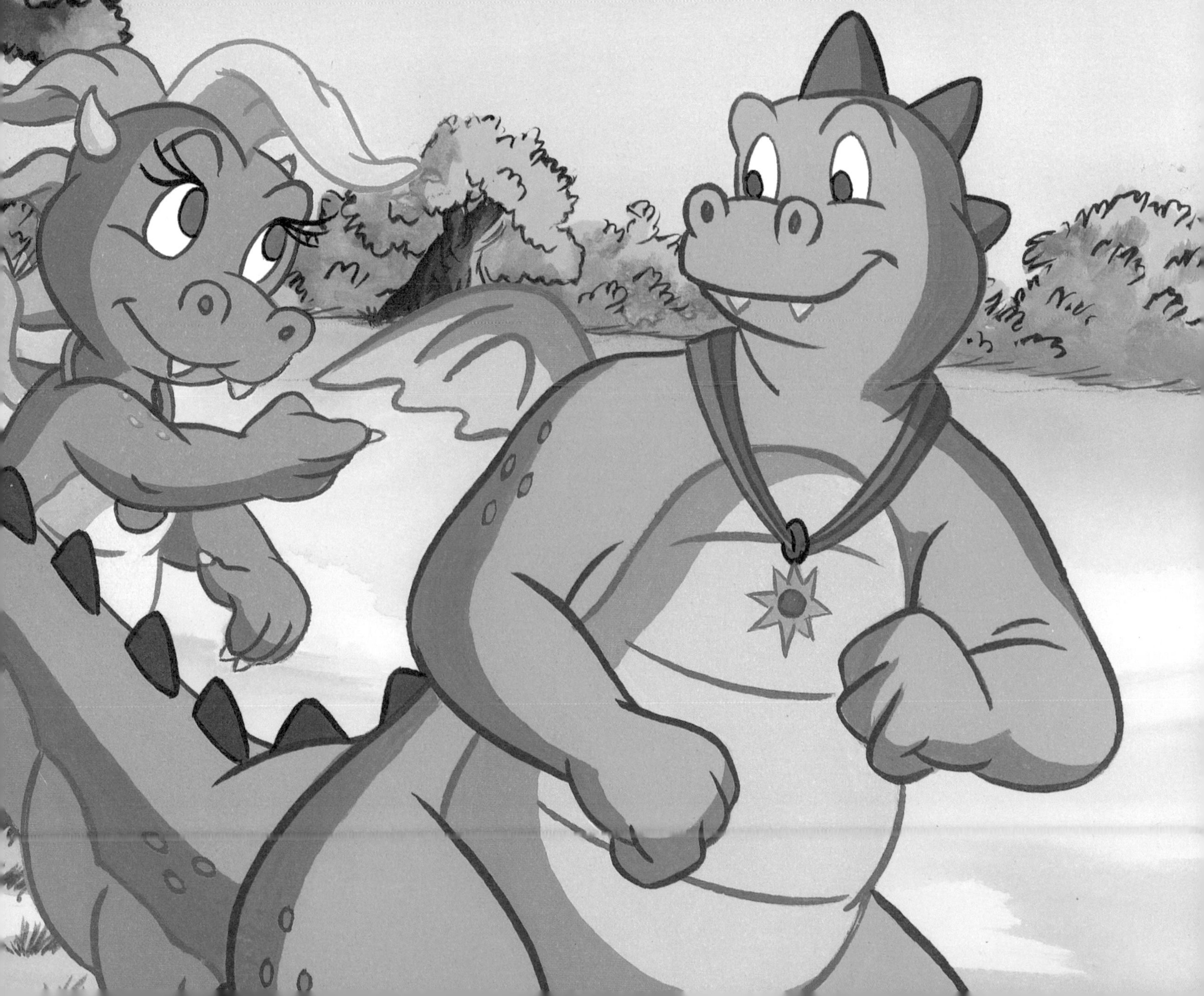

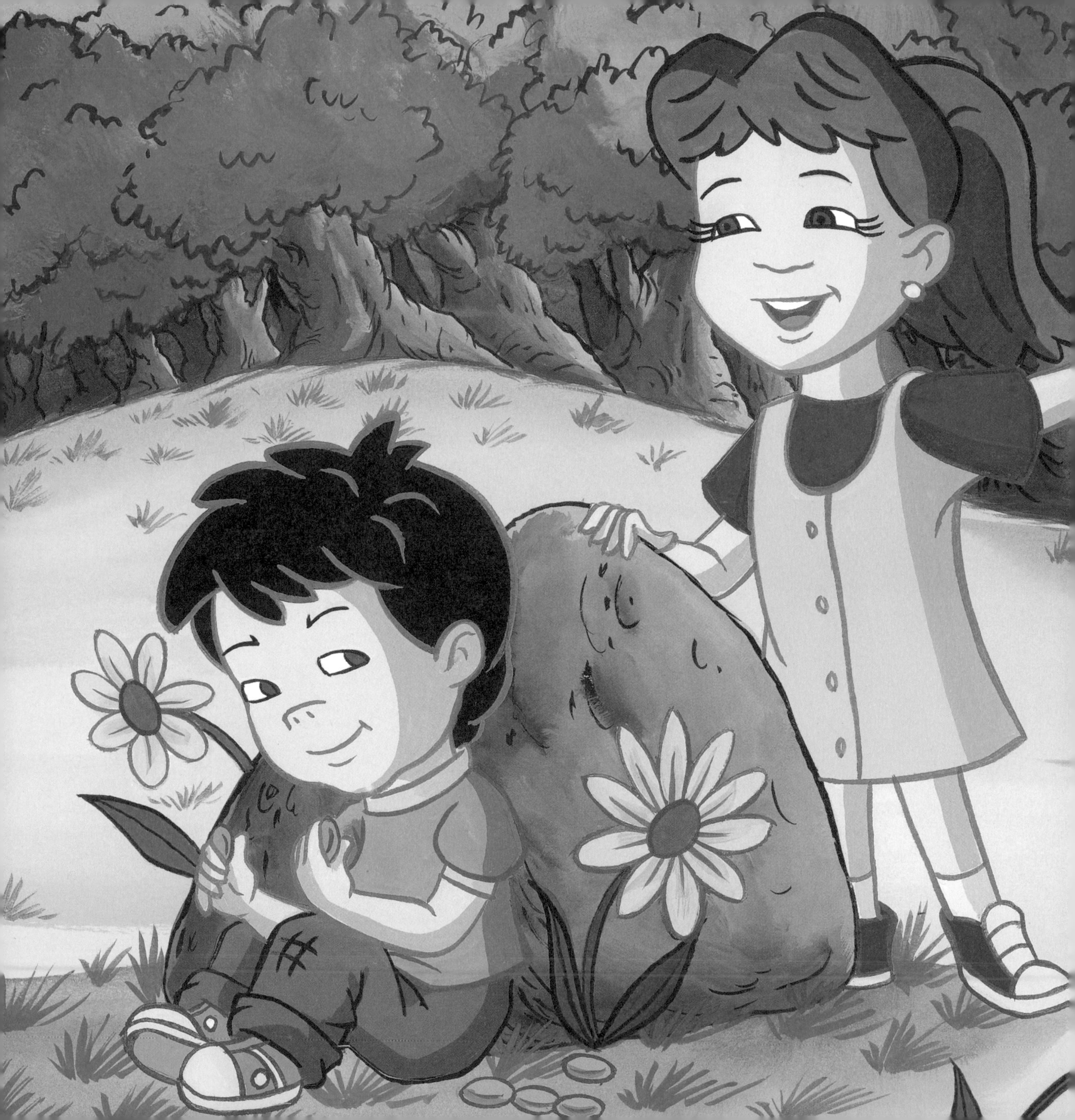

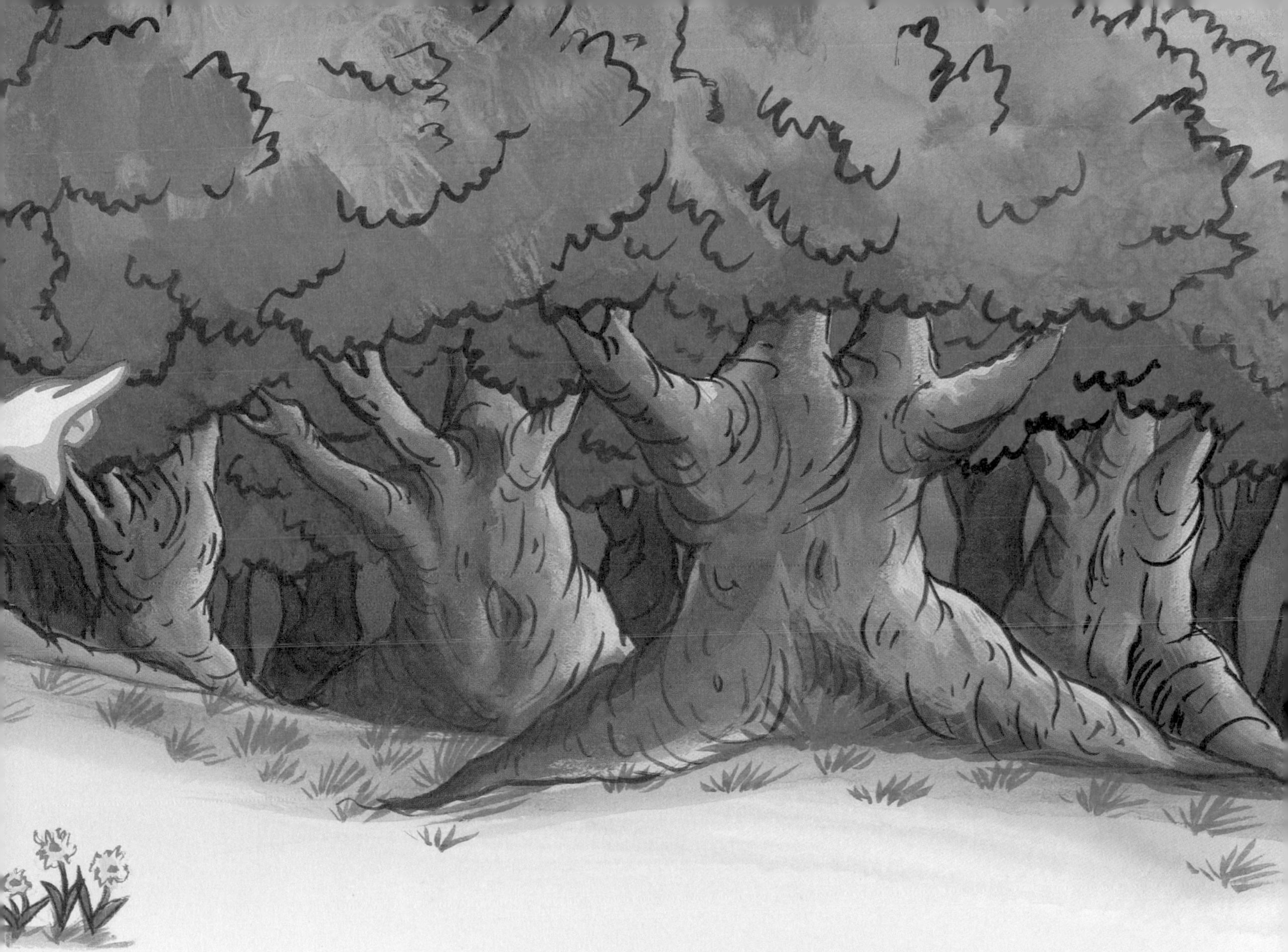

I bet they'd never find me in the Forest of Darkness, Emmy thought. But she knew she wasn't brave enough to go into the forest alone.

"Pssst, Max!" Emmy whispered. She pointed. "Let's hide in there."

Max hesitated. "It's too dark," he mumbled as he munched on some foofle flower seeds.

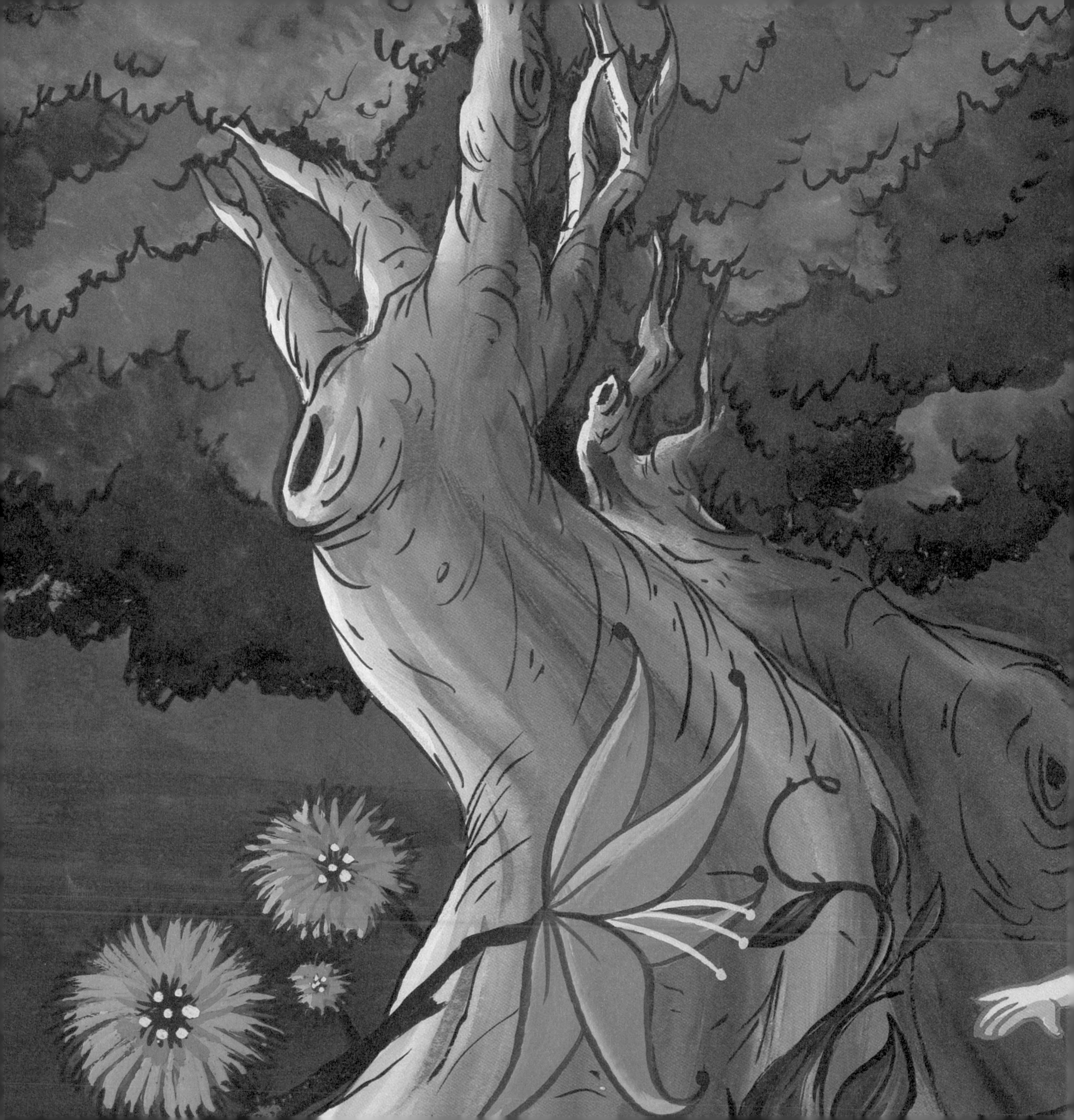